Marvellous Mummy

To my Mum - you rock my world... and to Oscar, Georgette and Darcy - thank you for making me a mummy.
Cuddle, cuddle, kiss xox. KP

To all the magnificent, amazing, awesome, spectacular, loving, gentle mothers in the world, especially my mum, Minda, my mother-in-law, Fran, and my own super star, Katie. GP

Marvellous Mummy

Katie Poli

Illustrated by Giuseppe Poli

NEW FRONTIER PUBLISHING

My mummy is silly and goofy and fun.

Tickle, tickle, squeeze.

My mummy is pretty and fancy and bright.

Sparkle, sparkle, shine.

My mummy is sneaky and quiet and still.

Tiptoe, tiptoe, creep.

My mummy is scary and noisy and loud.

Raah, raah, boo!

My mummy is happy and friendly and kind.

Wave, wave, smile.

My mummy is grumpy
and grouchy and cross.

Grumble, grumble, roar.

My mummy is clever and skilful and smart.

Think, think, fix.

My mummy is brave and daring and strong.

Jump, jump, swing.

My mummy is caring and gentle and sweet.

My mummy is cuddly and snuggly and warm.

Squish, squish, squeeze.

My mummy is perfect because
she is my mum.